"This is a novel about the electricity that inhabits us, sometimes predictably, sometimes like a lightning storm in the brain. It is also about a writer's relationship with her mother and about how fragile memory and language are. But above all it is about the terrible lucidity that comes with being abnormal, and how poetry is the only science that allows us to understand what someone like that sees."

—**Yuri Herrera, author of** *Ten Planets*

"The metamorphosis undertaken by Daniela Tarazona in *The Animal on the Stone* reaches its full form here, which, paradoxically, is not a form but rather its dissolution: a way of disappearing in words. The author has become writing. In her place, another woman who is pure language has left for an island with the intention of committing suicide. Or, rather, a woman—the same, another, which one, none— has not left for an island . . . I happen to understand and not understand this book. But it is in what I do not understand where I can best experience its atrocious lucidity as a chill of beauty and truth."

—**Luis Felipe Fabre, author of** *Recital of the Dark Verses*

"Closer to Lispector, Elizondo and Robbe-Grillet, as well as poetry as a concretion and reflection of the dissolution of the world, *Divided Island* traps us in its mystery without letting us out."

—**Ana García Bergua,** *Letras Libres*

"Daniela Tarazona's aesthetic appeals to the depths, to the power of evocation in literature. Magnificent, difficult, full of emotion and meaning."

—**Sara Poot Herrera, Andrea Jeftanovic, and Daniel Centeno Maldonado, Jury of the Sor Juana Inés de la Cruz Literature Prize 2022**

"It is the complexity of the writing of this book, its poetic dimension, that immerses us in the anxiety of living to such a degree that we want to die."

—**Adriana Pacheco,** *Hablemos Escritoras*

"This is writing to the limit, which is drawn on the sand of that island where Tarazona takes us and where we must allow ourselves to be led without logic or linearity, as when we are before a poem: surrendering ourselves to its mystery."

—**Alfredo Núñez Lanz,** *Literal Magazine*

Divided Island

Divided Island

Daniela Tarazona

TRANSLATED FROM THE SPANISH BY

LIZZIE DAVIS AND KEVIN GERRY DUNN

DEEP VELLUM PUBLISHING

DALLAS, TEXAS

Deep Vellum Publishing
3000 Commerce St., Dallas, Texas 75226
deepvellum.org · @deepvellum

Deep Vellum is a 501c3 nonprofit literary arts organization
founded in 2013 with the mission to bring
the world into conversation through literature.

Support for this publication has been provided in part by the National Endowment
for the Arts, the Texas Commission on the Arts, the City of Dallas Office of Arts and
Culture, the Communities Foundation of Texas, and the Addy Foundation.

ISBNs: 978-1-64605-314-8 (paperback) | 978-1-64605-329-2 (ebook)

LIBRARY OF CONGRESS CATALOGING-IN-PUBLICATION DATA
Names: Tarazona, Daniela, 1975- author. | Davis, Lizzie, 1993- translator.
| Dunn, Kevin Gerry, translator.
Title: Divided island / Daniela Tarazona ; translated from the Spanish by
Lizzie Davis and Kevin Gerry Dunn.
Other titles: Isla partida. English
Description: First US edition. | Dallas, Texas : Deep Vellum Publishing,
2024.
Identifiers: LCCN 2023046395 (print) | LCCN 2023046396 (ebook) | ISBN
9781646053148 (trade paperback) | ISBN 9781646053292 (ebook)
Subjects: LCSH: Brain damage--Fiction. | LCGFT: Psychological fiction. |
Novels.
Classification: LCC PQ7298.43.A73 I8513 2024 (print) | LCC PQ7298.43.A73
(ebook) | DDC 863/.7--dc23/eng/20231016
LC record available at https://lccn.loc.gov/2023046395
LC ebook record available at https://lccn.loc.gov/2023046396

Front Cover Design by Emily Mahon
Interior Layout and Typesetting by KGT

PRINTED IN CANADA

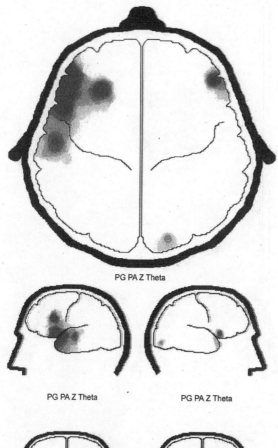

PG PA Z Theta

PG PA Z Theta

PG PA Z Theta

PG PA Z Theta

PG PA Z Theta

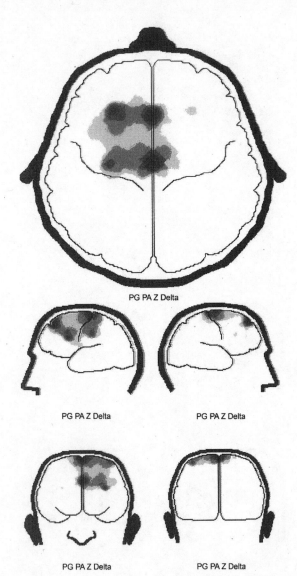

PG PA Z Delta

PG PA Z Delta

PG PA Z Delta

PG PA Z Delta

PG PA Z Delta

But surely in that first splendor was you,
and also in the deep rose, red, black,
flying ahead, faster even than light.

—MAROSA DI GIORGIO, *LA FLOR DE LIS*

Table of Contents

I.

CAREFUL WITH THE PEARLS

YOU OPEN THE FRONT DOOR. The light marks the coat of gray carpet in the living room. She's gone. In the kitchen, you examine the trash and establish her breakfast: eggshells rest atop rotting vegetable carcasses. The air clings to the smell of boiled water, you find a lit burner, the coil is glowing bright red.

You go into the bedroom, you don't look for her, knowing she's gone, but still, curiosity moves you; it's rare to be in someone else's house and free to contemplate her belongings, scrutinize traces: the comforter with the impression where she sat down—she changed shoes before leaving; the scent of the air she had breathed; the bathroom faucet, still dripping; the wet toothbrush. On a small bookshelf, her rings. She left with her hands bare forever.

You go back to the living room. Sit on the love seat. Look in all the corners like you might find something else there. Just one detail could make all the difference. There's a toy ball in the jumble of TV and telephone cables. (You remember she had a cat, Faustina, who ran away after one week.) At the other end of the room, under the bench where she placed three flowerpots, fraying carpet.

It's hot. You open the window to let in some air. Just then the phone rings. Her recorded voice informs the caller, correctly, that she isn't home. After the recording, a message.

"Hey, please call me when you're back."

The house is small and pierced by light. There's a number three hanging beside the front door. The whiteness of the walls is slightly blinding.

She must have left without anyone seeing. Maybe she peered through the window to make sure no one was walking around the courtyard. Maybe she even turned the key slowly so it wouldn't make a sound. For a long time, she had dreamed of leaving without being seen, you know that.

•

You stand and walk toward the door. The key is hanging in the lock. If the key is in your hand, how did she leave?

You hear the motors of idling cars while the light is red, then they go. She left early, an hour after sunrise. Wearing a green dress, the black shoes with ankle straps, hair pulled back into a ponytail. The street was almost empty, as expected. Just a red car, latest model, stopped at the light. Inside a man sat shaving with a device hooked up to the vehicle. The man did see her, glanced at her, but just kept going. She closed the door softly and left the building.

The sun is now in the center of the sky.

You hear the sound of the fridge, then go to the kitchen and open it. There are two large, full bottles of water, a jar of jam, a red ceramic butter tray. In the vegetable drawer: a head of garlic, an eggplant, an onion sprouting green shoots.

Three packets of instant oatmeal on the shelf beside the fridge.

You have to pee, so you go to the bathroom. The white shower curtain touches the floor, and you notice it's spotted with black—unmistakably mold from the dampness. You admire the tile floor, its geometric figures, the smallest is pink and the largest, dark purple; magnificent rhombuses unfolding on a white background.

That tile was once splattered with her blood. The day the wine made her fall. This story is also about the woman with the high forehead.

You look in the mirror over the sink. Where she put a sticker of a mandala. That mirror will hang on another wall, in another room, and reflect the face with the high forehead, the woman who will die. Across from the sink, you see two small flowerpots on the window ledge. In those plants lives the woman whose teeth stick out. If you look closely at the base of each plant, you will see her: there, the miniature woman, her body the size of a finger bone, is tending the earth, watering the flowerpots.

You flush the toilet. Your urine vanishes.

On the shelf, you see a jar of cream with DAY

AND NIGHT written on the lid in childlike hand-writing, followed by a small smiley face.

You go one room over. On the desk is her computer. A lucky find. It's the same scene you had dreamed. The interior of the machine makes you think of a body. It's obvious, but the metal pieces within, the slender cables, confirm the truth of the dream. This machine, you think, is where they uploaded her brain.

You turn and look at the study walls, which catch your eye because they're covered in Lotería cards. The sombrero, the devil, the dandy. They fill the space between shelves stacked two rows deep with books, almost collapsing.

Out the window, you see someone crossing the courtyard. A man, medium build, moving slowly, like his legs are hurt; his shoulders dance, one rises, the other falls. He has large sheets of cardboard under his arm, he's moving toward the street.

You go into the bedroom to hide. Sit on the bed, in her imprint, and look out the window facing the courtyard. You take your time getting your shoes off, as if you had all of eternity, and, slowly, you lie down; once your head is on the pillow, your feet come up. You place your hands on your abdomen, fingers laced, and gaze at the ceiling. The dampness has only gotten as far as the walls. Little by little, sleep comes. You drift off. You'll go toward the depths. She has only just left. She's traveling to the island.

•

The man you saw takes the cardboard boxes to the roof. He's standing up there, you could see him through the window if you were awake. He stacks up all the boxes and then, with a worn length of string, ties them together.

After eating the egg with a little salt, pepper, and lime, she throws the shell in the trash. She washes the cup she used as a bowl and puts it on the drying rack. Doesn't realize she left the burner on.

She stops in the kitchen doorway and looks at her hands. Closes them into fists as if testing her strength. She inhales deeply. Seems nervous.

Goes to the door. Turns the key, silently takes one more breath. Something disturbing is waiting outside.

Peers out just before crossing the threshold, makes sure no one's there, at that moment, walking around in the courtyard. Leaves her house. Doesn't look back. Pulls closed the handle. Goes, with no coat. Two pearls adorn her ears.

SUPERIMPOSITIONS

TEN PEOPLE ARE LINED UP at the latrine. Next is you. You go in, crouch, strain to defecate. Down below, on the far side of the orifice where the waste drops, are humpback whales. When you finish, you wipe with beige paper whose cylinder hangs from a wire.

Outside, the person behind you in line has gone.

Summer afternoon has arrived in an immense city.

Now you walk along the street and are met with that foul odor: vapors rise from the manholes.

You get to the next crosswalk. The red car, latest model, hits a pole. The driver dies.

You sit on the sidewalk to wait. You want to see if the ambulances will get there fast or slow; it doesn't matter, anyway, if they're slow.

A few minutes pass. Pedestrians stop, like you, to watch what's happening. The foul smell from the manholes now seems more intense, maybe it's the smell of death.

The paramedics hurry out of the ambulance. One of them uses a mallet to smash in the driver's side window. Then he leans in half his body, comes out, declares: He's dead. Goes in again, searches the dead man, then says, through his living body: His name was Serafín.

You stand. Look up and see, high above, an enormous blimp floating in the air. It's branded with the name of the world's most famous soft drink (which you then read): COCA-COLA. She bursts into your thoughts, the woman with restless eyes who left for the island. She, in fact, is you.

•

Two hours have passed since you fell asleep. When you wake up, you feel refreshed. The sewer smell was there because it had to be, you think.

You remember you witnessed an accident on the highway not long ago, and the boy who died, just fifteen or sixteen years old, had the same name as the driver in your dream: Serafín.

You go to the kitchen and fill a glass with water. Look through the window at the color of the sky. It's going to be a spectacular afternoon.

You close your eyes and think of your mother, who is no longer in this world.

Something you told her when she was dying:

"The property, Mom, it's so beautiful with the trees you planted, they're huge now."

"That was a good thing to do," she replied from her death place.

She had wanted the stretch of earth along the street to be thick with pines.

Once, those trees had burned in the flames of a wildfire.

As kids, you would search for pre-Hispanic artifacts there, in the freshly worked earth. And you'd find them: shattered pots, obsidian arrowheads, small clay faces, encircling holes dug by moles who chewed at the roots of the plants.

Then, lodged in your socks, you found peculiar, round, spiny-edged seeds that pricked your ankles.

·

Faced with the memories and her death, you extend threads from your temples, a proxy for reaching what's no longer there, what no longer is, and you fail. It makes you angry.

And you asked her, as she was leaving:

"Give me your hand, let me warm it up a little."

She extended her left hand. You had never experienced cold like that. Took it between your own hands and cradled it like a strange baby. Her nails shone bright, were alive.

·

Talk about the link between earth and sky. Say: If we'd wanted to, Mother, together we could have dissolved our entire surroundings. Your powers, almighty, could have made ghosts of the furniture,

26

of the walls. Maybe they did, and I was just incapable of seeing.

.

Maybe the employees at the funeral home turned my body on the bed, and there rushed from my mouth a grotesque black liquid, à la Madame Bovary. Then they might've taken me feet-first to prepare for the wake.

It's true that you went to her wardrobe and took out the coral silk dress she had shown you months earlier. You thought she wanted to wear it that day. You knew—it was a superimposition.

You could have opened the window so her spirit would exit freely. Could have lit a candle.

"Please, even a small flame," you could have said in a whisper.

Just before she died, she asked when you would quit smoking, and you went to get a cigarette to show to her, to smoke later on the balcony, a slight.

State the manner of panic, the voice of terror. Approach the scream and grab it with your mouth to make it heard. Right now you're shouting. You shout with so much force your jugular vein pops out.

·

It's pain. The gaze settled on trees seeks meaning. You think you need to hit upon meaning; that is, you think there are things with meaning. For instance: there's a portrait in oil of you with a star on your forehead.

·

The effort will not be in vain.

•

With the first split, there were no voices. There have never been voices, just fast-stacking thoughts, one almost on top of another. Nor are there jaws, and the lack of a mouth makes the horror unbearable.

You open the palms of your hands: there, the small copper-red stains. Pooled blood. There was once a woman who told you: Those stains are the mark of a fatal disease.

•

The surgery took a long time. The doctors say she's doing okay. Your mother's head is shaved. She looks more German than before. They say they took out most of the tumor. Most. The rest, they couldn't get.

You were with her at the hospital so many times.

"We should document her case," a specialist says. "I've never seen anyone handle chemo the way she does."

•

(They left. They'd been there behind you for many nights and days while your mother was sick. Monitored your actions, your commute to and from work, your correspondence, your phone calls, your writing, your forward slant when you walk. They kept track of all that. What you don't know is why.)

•

The light this Monday afternoon is gentle. What you mean is: there are clouds you're able to see across the whole sky. Everyone you pass on your way to the taxi stand exhibits the usual resignation of a person alive on a Monday. They work, have good manners, expect nothing of the day except its passage. Expect things to go peacefully, for the day to be mostly kind to the majority, to their customers, also to the women leaving their homes.

A friend once told you anyone could be crazy;

"everybody's a little off in the head," he said, "maybe your case is just more visible." Your too-big eyes, the way you speak—sometimes your voice breaks and you don't know why. Relative to the visible, then, you could argue that the invisible is even more interesting. Say, for example: imagine what my brain holds. Let's dream something up: yesterday and the day before I had good dreams. In one of them I was saying my name. My name is the same as it was in the dream.

•

You were thinking it before, where did she go?

She's gone.

Talk about her scent. Say she smelled like an endangered animal, and also like moisturizer.

She had washed her face, as usual, the day she left for the island. You left hand-in-hand with her, became an extension of her body.

Hold your hands in your lap to halt a little of yourself, and so she doesn't completely escape. Shield is the word. Let her shield and give you precisely the breath you need to name what you've seen.

Once upon a time there was the sun. Seething sphere. If the word were she, it meant you; you were replicated. Her over you. You over her. Two bodies spinning in circles.

"Look closely," you said. Legs turned to arms. Head always a hindrance to legs and to hands, ancient goddess looking around.

•

The world looks like them, the ones chasing you. If you accept the advice, you exert the force of the mask. Put one on, said a man, just like everyone else. And you put hers on; with a mask, you breathe easier. You see other people's faces overlapping, too, and you feel a little better, with your own mask. You don't want to be human. Say it, enunciate it, don't be part of the species that annihilates other souls. Don't be that.

"Here I am," you say. And you add: "I am not human."

•

Come afternoon, the sun will vanish behind the invisible horizon; the buildings occupy its line. The city trembles. The buildings empty of bodies. She'll travel by plane.

A middle-aged man with a bundle of herb-of-grace passes her. The same man who once brushed her back and her legs with a bundle like that.

The multiplicity of thoughts has its cost. She counted the bills; she'd been saving to go read the letters the following month. But it doesn't make sense anymore. She won't do it.

•

The new substance has given you luminous dreams, you fall in love, it's subtle; as if slowly kissing your mouth, the substance seduces and pilfers, despite you, your memories. You want to transmit the terrible former agony, the days when you were chased, but they're over. Now an acidic nostalgia floods you. On the radio, not one more

sentence that might allude to that chase. The terror has disappeared, as if by magic.

It's possible others look at you thinking
you're unwell. That doesn't matter either. Within
you resides a feeling deeper than apathy. There's
been a prolonged period of suffering. The fall, the
collapse, the scream, the cruel solitude. On the
other side of horror, a void: the transparency of
facts, imbalance swapped for a chemical softness
that devours your torturous thoughts. You were
the sea.

•

How does one live believing in nothing?
Sometimes you yield to the light. You're suscep-
tible to beauty. Sunlight is one example. Then
you lose that ability. Instead, you look around to
confirm that perceptions deceive: nothing that
happens matters. We resist by constructing illu-
sions. We bow our heads so another can come
and sever them.

If you were to dream of the atom bomb, just

like you did as a child, this time you'd watch it fall. Speak what is certain. The world is going to end.

Your cousin Rafael has a small garden at his house. He also believes the world could end. The portent of ruin prompted him to plant tomatoes and beets. The only way to live unpoisoned is to eat what the earth provides. The staples are grown by abuse. In a pot that you yourself tend, the produce is ideal.

Were you born reading it all to the point of exhaustion?

The doctor asked: When you were a kid, did you have an overactive imagination?

THE WOMAN ON THE ISLAND

The island where she's headed appeared on the sea after an underwater volcano had erupted.

When her relocation begins, she feels a navel-height emptiness. She left the house, the old neighborhood, because she knows she can't go on living. Doesn't feel like it. On the days leading up to her leaving, she thought of surviving, but that was confusion. Visited her friend, the least qualified one to accompany her on the passage to death, waited, not speaking to anyone, walked to the end. Prepared nothing, gave no notice, thought it needless. Took leave of unknown matters within herself, as a mute person would.

If she'd been buried when she died, she would have gone in a common grave.

Now she's holding the red carry-on, six garments. The island is uninhabited. She can spend the afternoon there and die later, when night falls and the stars are visible. She has the bag of pills. Has the photo of her mother, her father's words wound around her ears.

She sits with her hands crossed in her lap. From above, she examines the gray avenue the taxi takes to the airport. She's dizzy from not eating, cold, her fingers like red sausages, blood pooled. It's summer; still, she's cold.

Months ago she took a trip to another country. But that isn't to say the world has given her opportunities. She looked around, surprised by the places she managed to visit, but they didn't matter enough for her not to die. The people she stayed with on that journey were probably distraught to learn she had died by her own hand.

The woman is young and present for her conclusion. She will be witness to and origin of her demise. Maybe it's the most selfish act a person can commit. Being your own executioner, eluding what others consider natural death. Seizing your one and only death.

In the known world, living has become an

unbearable task. For years astrologers have prophesied a dark era for humanity, stretching far into the future. These days anything's for sale. Ideas bought up like commodities. Emotions exchangeable for cash.

The woman doesn't want to continue. She's been driven by hope to believe in alien life, has fixed her spirits to the nourishing idea of reincarnation, is now proficient at adapting to reality, but none of it is enough; again and again, she's repelled. Anyone who knows her personality, what they call character, could confirm that her suffering is intrinsic, constitutional, and the sentence would be set in the wall of truth to serve as her gravestone. Her body may know how it feels to be buried alive, trapped between bricks; within a terrifying wall, she breathes still, out of panic.

She is several women. Embodies the aching lives of escapists who rebelled from the very start and found it impossible to achieve flames. Like the ones who resisted ruination and were reborn, only to then find themselves immersed, again, in horror. Though they know the eternal condition of existence: onward to ruination for one and all, some less distressed than others, some lost in the senselessness.

This woman, then, represents multitudes. Her passing is not circumstantial, nor is it irrelevant: as she reaches her conclusion, so do uncountable eyes outside their orbits: unbearable, supremely intelligent gazes snuffed out when they failed to withstand terrestrial life. Humanity now purges and exterminates, does away with whoever fails to adapt to its use-and-disposal procedure. She is power, candor, her words rise above the others' heads like prayers, and thus she finds herself out of place. Voices that declare themselves, that ascend ever higher, aren't welcome now. The aim is productive exchange, which strips the word of its meaning. She'll fall silent to die with dignity.

YOU MOVE IN THAT DIRECTION

You were hemming pants when, through your bedroom window, you saw a flash of light that instantly became a ball of fire. You swallowed hard. There was no doubt about it, you'd just seen a UFO with your own two eyes. A UFO! You ran to tell your siblings, grabbed their arms and pulled them to your room, sat them down to wait for the unbelievable to repeat itself, but no. It didn't happen again.

You wrote it down in your notebook: Today I saw a UFO out my bedroom window. And that's all. You didn't tell Aunt Clementina, the only person who would have believed you.

You had decorated your desk with sheets of colored paper where you copied down sentences from books to get a hold on them. The desk, too, was a spacecraft of sorts, with shelves above your head. To travel, you stuck almost half your body inside.

The E.T. poster—glowing finger, eyes looking straight at the camera—was a reminder that freedom existed. If an extraterrestrial could, unabashed, show the world his glowing finger, was anything impossible?

Strange things were happening at home. Your mother kept saying her things had disappeared, asking if someone had moved them, only to find them returned to their places shortly thereafter.

Strangest of all during that period was the transferring of Christ's face. On the landing hung a portrait of Jesus your grandmother had given your older brother. When they took it down to replace the wallpaper with white paint, his whole face remained: eyes, cheeks, chin, hair. A disaster, or the opposite. Nothing. Humidity doing experiments with the paintings in the house.

Also, at a church in our neighborhood, Our Lady of Guadalupe appeared on one of the outside walls. People came with prayers of petition and left flowers, which they hung on a rod driven into the stone.

•

The ceiling in your room was made of bricks and beams. On one of the bricks, you could see a dog's pawprint. Just a single pawprint.

When you were little, you and your siblings used to play superheroes. Your uniform sweaters were capes. And they jumped the fence between the yard and the quarry and cried out in triumph.

"My daughter has leukemia, anything helps."

"I don't have change," you said.

"Here, I do," he replied.

This world is made up of symbolic acts. He brought a phone to his ear. His daughter was a victim of abuse. The words "leukemia" and "change" had suggested as much, you thought.

A worthy act: when you looked in his eyes, an industrial force sucked the fear from your brain, as if the man's red gaze contained all the power of a superior vacuum cleaner. If ever you find yourself beside a car with a name like a vacuum, understand that a stealthy and terrible force has decided to gulp down whatever it likes of your insides.

•

You should have written the visions down. Now the details are gone.

•

The man who saw you from the street, who lifted his hand, was also perverse. Someone had let him know that you would be there at that precise moment. So lifting his hand meant knowing that you agreed with them. A stranger's gesture of solidarity.

Danger of death.

•

Your mother came out of the bathroom, washed her hands thoroughly, and then pulled some lip gloss from her purse. She ran it over her upper lip three times and her bottom lip twice, starting in the middle and working her way out. Then she pressed them together and rubbed until the pink gloss was well distributed.

The first time you saw her do a headstand, you

felt a profound astonishment. You were dazzled by the ease with which she lifted her legs toward the ceiling. From that position, she spoke to you: Come on, I'll teach you, she said. But you never learned. Standing on your head is a serious matter, you must have thought, with your characteristic formality. Your mother did yoga so adeptly that she later became an instructor.

One morning they left for Chapultepec Park. They were going to meet with the Swami, El Camarón. His disciples were a multitude. Everyone had to bring food. Your grandmother made sandwiches, your mother made a salad. They ate there under the trees, the noise of traffic audible. There was bread. Your grandmother said the loaves multiplied, exclaimed with admiration: The Swami made more bread, did you see? There wouldn't have been enough. He did it without a word, that's his way. That's just how he is.

They wanted to live better.

.

The sinks in the bathroom off your room at the Cuernavaca house were exquisite: two seashells, and the water jetted out from the mouths of bronze seahorses. The room's spaciousness inspired you to breathe deeply and walk proudly, boasting about it to classmates who hadn't ever come over but whose visits you imagined. You had a porch, a front-row seat to the downpours.

That day, your grandmother wouldn't talk about her extraordinary abilities. You insinuated something while the two of you sat on the porch watching the sunset, but she changed the subject.

She talked about her trip to India.

"When you go, unscrew your head when you land. Nothing you know will be of any use there."

•

You were Gretel and your cousin Manuel was Hänsel; each of you performed with all your might. It was the second time your grandmother made you act. The summer before, you'd put on *A Midsummer Night's Dream* at the family houses.

Since there were more cousins than characters, your grandmother wrote you some lines. You were the morning star, a wig of silver wire on your head.

How can a story cross immense oceans?

What does it mean to eat while people on nearby corners keep watch? Did you see them?

The games perversity plays are obvious any time of day. At its zenith, the sun lights up millions of loathsome exchanges.

You can't talk about the magic. There's no way. Mouth opens, hands write, to say: magic is. Death is upon you.

·

"I know you, but I can't remember where from," an old man said to you, desiring the body next to him in the café, a beautiful young woman. By no means would her body undress for the old man's eyes.

The scrambled egg was still in your esophagus. Indigestible, you thought.

"I think I'm going to die," you could have said right then, across from your friend, in the café.

Everything meant something else. The apple no longer an apple.

If a beloved family member were in danger, you were to go to a café with the name of his destiny. Oh, but you thought that too late. The street was where your death could take place. You lived inside a prison of astonishing proportions.

He's not in danger anymore, you thought. Your act had the right address. It was nice getting coffee here.

TABLEAU OF WONDERS

AT THE BACK OF THE landscape, there's a sunset.
A yellow bird flies on top of an orange sky. The
main figure in the tableau is a mule made out of
palm fronds, he's carrying grains of rice painted
blue, set upon a ground adorned with the words:
SEASON'S GREETINGS. Behind that is an ear of
wheat, beside which sits an emerald, a tiny prism,
a miniature basket. To the right, a gilded owl, eyes
wide open, staring. From the ceiling hangs a miniature Santa Claus blown in red glass, apparently
climbing down a thin string, empty-handed—it's
St. Nick, your mother would say. At the edge: a silver charm, a sun and moon connected. Below that
hangs the face of a shaman, dirty and silver plated,
with a black bead glued to his neck. There's also
a paper broom in a corner, standing on its head.

Above the owl, crocheted together with red and white yarn, a pearl and an amber bead.

At the bottom of the tableau, the background is embellished with a small floral dish, beside it: another emerald, raw; a white dove; a triangular tiger's-eye bead; and a yellow cat decal watching the scene, somber or incredulous, no telling which. To the left, a minute porcelain vase, black flowers painted on the base, pink ones higher up; beside it, a little white egg whose cracked shell has been pieced back together.

•

It turns out you're surrounded, you're an island with water on all sides: the reams of paper by the desk, the books, the suitcase of jewelry. Your mother's things. Notes. Letters. Your grandmother's manuscripts.

Strange things happen to you. The decorations in that tableau of wonders, seem to accurately describe the moment you're living in: you've got an orange tabby; the porcelain plates your mother painted arrive at the house; you wrote a novel about a woman who lays an egg. The tableau existed before the novel. Does the order in which things happen in time really matter? Being surrounded means sinking in sand. Your body gets lost among objects, you can barely open your eyes. Seeing is a state of grace, here, right now.

Your mother's absence is more painful as time passes. You need her. Her death must be a lie. She gave the tableau to you for your birthday.

It happened like this: she was sitting, looking out at the horizon crowded with buildings.

"There," she said, eyes wide open. "It was real." That's when the bombs fell. She decided to leave for the island. And left.

•

The photo you're holding now, of your grandfather on your mother's side, shows the scars from the shrapnel, the genetically floppy outer ears, the prominent contour of his lips. On the fabric of his jacket, you can make out the shimmer of dust. Other bombs fell beside him.

You'll chew fruit without teeth from now on, just like you saw your grandfather do at the nursing home. Madre del Carmen, that was the place.

Chew the fruit without using your teeth, do it right now. Your bare gums. Top lip sunk into your face. Hands on your knees. Talk about The Dogs of War, the book your grandfather read. Say: It's a story. Chew cherries with your gums and toss the pits behind the furniture like he did.

Let an old woman roll past in a wheelchair, a bottle held to her mouth with one gaunt hand.

Now you're at the bedroom door, you're an old woman, but your hips still sway when you walk. You look at the old man in front of you, say: You're just the same as always, pointing your finger at everyone else.

Erase yourself immediately from the scene, you're no longer the happy, lively old woman.

•

Wind.

•

The archangel with the sword in one hand and

the scales in the other, who is it? It's your maternal grandmother, the old woman who persisted. It's Saint Michael the Archangel, at the Last Judgment. He's weak, though, and small. Really, Supreme Commander of Heavenly Hosts?

·

Say: Grandpa, on the wall of your cousin's house, there's a Velázquez. You saw it with your brother. The house was abandoned, its only inhabitants two basset hounds from England.

In the bathroom you saw a tortoiseshell comb, a beauty of a comb.

Pigeons came in through the gaps in the roof. The furniture was all the color of bird shit.

"Let's get out of here," you said.

You went out to the garden, struggled through the undergrowth, toward the gate, then exited onto Avenida del Libertador.

·

Your grandfather used to get up at dawn to meditate. He would sit on a leather stool where he had placed a green-and-white plaid blanket, hand woven, and wrap himself up in rabbit furs. His room had rounded walls and orange carpeting, orange just like his teacher was always wearing, the Swami, El Camarón.

You usually slept in the low-ceilinged room that was next to his: the burrow. The blankets weighed on your body. You were even smaller then, and sometimes, sleeping there, you'd slam your fist against the wall and wake up with scraped knuckles.

SHE GOES TOWARD THE ISLAND

The seat she's traveling in has given way, she shifts her body as she can to avoid the springs under the fabric.

In the last photo of her you will see, she's tilting her body forward in the car of a Ferris wheel. She's alone but someone, whoever is taking the photo, is with her.

Now her eyes are closed; her head, against the window. Shortly, the plane will take off. She'll sleep because getting this far has cost her countless sleepless nights and many days of fitful eating. Her exhaustion stems from enduring the endless wakefulness and elective undernourishment, her body's death wish.

She's afraid. Has enthusiastically researched the pills' effects, whether they'll cause too much pain, and concluded they will. She summons courage. The physical pain, plus the sadness she has carried since she can remember, will amount to less than the pain of her soul, and with tears, she will withstand death's deprivations.

Now she's reading about a piano teacher who falls in love with her student. The author is vicious with her characters. The piano teacher shares a bed with her mother and finds herself debilitated by love. She wounds her own body, seems to relish the knife's incisions, or rather, finds in them, made palpable, the damage life deals her each day. The piano teacher in the novel reminds her of herself.

She has forged this move toward death on her own, she can't be a victim because she assumes, taking characteristic responsibility, that her heart has determined her situation and destiny. That is: she accepts the emotional deficit that has caused her to suffer over time, bestows a yes—honest and fed by her breath—to the inclemency of her existence.

Abruptly, she thinks of the naked body of the

last person she loved. Shoulder blades jutting out high on his back, collarbone upholding that boyish face. If she had been able to, she would have loved him for years. But the idea of dying pulsed in her like breath: a need that would, at last, be fulfilled. Recalling the way he would look at her bare breasts, she feels her eyes grow moist and then, with reluctance, release one thick tear that falls on the page of the book in her hands, which almost always reveal her poor circulation.

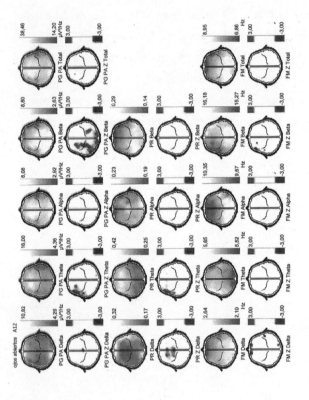

Age: 39.07

Record date: 21 July 2014

EF exhibits left frontotemporal hyperexcitability

II.

A FLOWER ON HIS BROW

Eunice is setting the table. She'll have dinner with Olga, your grandmother. Proper nouns are a rabbit punch. There's chicken in the oven, juicy, the aroma of browning meat permeating the living room, bedrooms sunk in crimson curtains.

It's not the right time to pee, but Eunice is in the bathroom. The flower out front, a poinsettia they hung from the door, is fake. Olga adjusts her earrings. "Hoops," she says, "I'm adjusting my hoops." It's early. Elena will be there later, with gringo poets. They went for a walk downtown. She had wanted to show them the throngs that fill her eyes with water. Wherever she looks becomes an acid curtain.

Eunice sits in the light-blue chair in the living room. The chair's wings make her look like someone emerged victorious. Her red hair stands out against the fabric, coarse, thick, luminous. Olga is across from her.

It's not just women who show up. I'm writing about when Lee Harvey Oswald had dinner at a house in Colonia Roma, in Mexico City.

Lee Harvey Oswald enters the scene. His hands are in his pockets—of course. Lee has hands that could be deadly. Revealed, they look like steel hooks. Lee has the face of a lost animal, and he is one. The house strikes him as enormous, but only because of his bristling nerves.

He stretches his arms toward something few people notice: a pair of long antlers. Lee is both man and caribou. A flower sprouts from his wide forehead the moment he enters the house. Flowers grow slowly, as we know. So Lee brings one hand to his forehead and breathes, precise, confident, calm. At this instant, the petals of the plant are two small buds.

Olga places one hand on her heart when she

sees Lee come in. She couldn't say why she does this, it's automatic, like blinking, but the motion arises from a white-hot inner force. Behind Lee are Samuel and Benjamin, two more poets. They're just as odd in that house as he is. Eunice speaks: "Please, sit down," while Olga watches Lee from the corner of her eye, penetrating and wary. Something about him makes her brash, even a little flushed in certain areas of her body. It's not just the heat. It's his hands like hooks, the way his hair falls on his forehead. It's the train of his shadow in the hallway.

Now it's late, and the chicken is getting cold. Eunice basted it with the drippings so it would glisten. A roast chicken should rattle the table.

Lee scratches the flower that grows from his forehead. Your grandmother thinks of her tongue in that mouth, or in the mouth of her beloved— the same mouth she lusts after now. Benjamin and Samuel only speak English, so the conversation bends in two directions: toward Eunice, who handles the language with ease, and Olga, who misses much of what she hears. But Lee speaks

Spanish, he has a good accent. The corners of his mouth have turned orange and shiny with chicken grease.

By now there's a reddish protuberance on Lee's forehead, a bud about to bloom, the heliconia that will take his brow in the end.

Olga looks at Lee's forehead and notices the protuberance. It doesn't strike her as strange, since nothing about this man is unfamiliar to her. She'd take his organs, for example, if this were another story. She would feed his flesh, she would be him.

Lee's antlers are blocking part of the painting in the room, a portrait of Olga done by Rodolfo Zanabria; no one, except for her, has taken notice of the antlers, imposing and covered in the finest fuzz, like moss the color of wheat. Olga's face in the painting, then, has Lee's horns at just this moment.

The diners keep silent.

When Lee looks down to grab his napkin, the horns reach as far as Olga's upturned nose, which grazes the fuzz and the strange creation those horns represent. Lee, the caribou man, touches his forehead and feels something burst like a boil, except it's the flower, the buds that emerged from his skin.

THE WOMAN FROM THE STORY

She reached the desert, lips blistered by thirst. The thoughts multiplied. Followed behind her. Strangers too close. Her hands now hung near her body, downed. Belly filled with suspicions. Everyone lies. No one tells the truth, she thought. The suffering hasn't ended because there's a deep wound there now, in the place that's also the source of thoughts, angst, insatiable electricity. Maybe the wound was there before she was born. The doctor told her it might be a scar in her brain's smooth gray matter. Then they asked her to do the study. They ended up realizing the electricity was scattering this way and that, dysrhythmias of unknown origin. The pain is prehistoric. The hand reaching out for another hand is historic.

•

She looked up to search for the exit. Where was the desert door? On this divided island? She sunk her feet in the sand to confirm she was there. There's no question that she saw a woman. The only one who held out her hand. The woman from the story.

She and you are the same person. It doesn't matter that you each inhabit a different body. Conjugations are irrelevant. Says she and says you. The woman who left for the island is she and you.

•

The lightning that discharged at the crown of your head is millenarian, ancestral, formless, forceful. A light beyond words came to you.

Head shattered on the ground, brains split and phosphorescent, hand politely at the chest, hair scorched. Then look at all of it through a kaleidoscope. A riot of light. Who knows if you'll symbolize the lightning one day.

•

Rest.

Wake up.

Wake up.

It's almost time for the walnuts. Walnuts will rain down on the cars and pedestrians. But they won't hurt anyone. At last, the fruit of Heaven will fall from the sky. It's about time.

The desert is a crossing point. From here, she'll go to another outlandish place, it's safe to say, but she'll also find the tree with metallic leaves, and at its foot, a star in the grass. Light will shine all around the frame of a closed door. The star won't be the wake of any spacecraft, but the sign that she has arrived in a new kingdom.

•

At the start of the trip, waiting for her taxi, the one on the island saw an old woman walk down the street. She was with her daughter. Her eyes showed recent shock. Captivity returns: the woman now

depended on her daughter. Imprisoned, she goes
for a walk to see how time passes. The edges of
things aren't as sharp as they were in her youth:
they now show the degradation of the years. Maybe
the things in her house are new, furniture from
an upscale department store, carpets frequently
cleaned, vases brandishing dignified petals. But
even in all that, the old woman sees the end is near.
Death is approaching, will pass through matter,
death will cross walls to arrive at her neck, slim and
covered in creases, to drink her blood. That's how
it will be, thought the woman on the island, when
she at last reached the coast.

•

Your great-aunt Lara taught you to use an eraser.
Ever since, you've held the sheet of paper with the
index finger and thumb of one hand and used the
other to rub the eraser over a word to make it vanish. You've erased the word *love*.

•

To tell another story, you have to remember Olga, your grandmother, driving her compact car. She was going up a hill. (Across from the hill there's a shopping mall now.) The ascent was definitive, she was still young, but she was headed toward her end. A voice whose origin she couldn't pinpoint let out a shriek that made her stop and reconsider. Then she pulled over, left the motor running, and thought about going back.

•

You're alive.

Your memory is bad. You almost never remember names, but theirs you remember.

And also the blue fingernails on your sick grandmother Olga.

"To kill himself, the writer ran tubes from his nose to the gas stove. Mm. I thought it was such a wonderful way to die. I even went to town, got some rubber tubes myself. For years, I kept them under my bed," she says.

•

If you open the kitchen door at your grand-mother's house, and then the wooden door that keeps the flies from her, you'll find her in the gar-den. She's bent over, pulling weeds.

"Should I heat up the rabbit?" you ask.

She plunges into the water. Before her eyes is Isla de la Iguana. Her body finds itself surrounded by liquid. She's an island of flesh and bone that will sink later on. In her eyes an image forms: her mother's smiling face, she knows those teeth, that way of looking, lost in madness.

·

Sketch a circle with more circles inside.

Keep telling the story. She finally got to the island. A man in a small boat took her. A one-way trip. She'll stay forever. Until her body swells with putrefactive gases and even after: until her flesh goes and only her bones remain.

You gave away the ending.

•

Your cat has just leapt onto the desk: a bug is flying up against the ceiling, he wants to trap it.

•

She gets off the boat and says goodbye to the fisherman.

"So you don't want me to come back for you?"

"No, that's all right, thank you."

Maybe days will pass. She'll hallucinate from hunger. Skin undone by the sunlight. Thirst. She'll die quickly.

Before she arrived at the island, she had breakfast at a restaurant near the port. Ordered pancakes, bacon, a coffee. She had spent the three previous nights at a boarding house. A spacious room with a twin bed and yellow curtains; the ceiling fan meowed like a kitten.

The flight from city to port was like any other. You're surprised by how events transpire identically. She stared out the window the whole time, as if she might find something special at that altitude. Nothing.

The morning she left her house, she had forgotten to turn off the burner. The day before that, she had gone to work. She didn't say she'd be leaving. Her hands were bare, ringless.

A month earlier, on a hot night, she had dreamed of the island. Saw herself naked, alone, sloughed off in the sand like a snail's shell, eroded by water, wind, salt. In the dream, she ran her tongue along her pursed lips to taste the salt. It was there.

She knew exactly what facts had carried her to the journey.

·

Her hair is matte. The sand made rough tangles. Eyes sunken in a famished face. Hands like lobsters, like spiders: fingertips buried in sand, phalanges jutting out. The word is "fraying."

She has no breasts. Her nipples are two purple blotches.

•

Mention the rays that you saw, and that she saw before you, a while ago. Waking up and noticing strange beams of light in the bedroom. Where are they coming from? Say you asked where the light was coming from. Don't be afraid. It doesn't matter if Saint Michael the Archangel is watching you from the bookshelf. Your mother had him restored. What for? The archangel's hands were empty: he had wings but no sword or scales. His face had faded. The mouth is vanishing into his yellowish skin even now. Restored, he has pink wings, they look like the leaves of a tree but with light-blue nervation, they're made of spongy wood and might float in the bathroom sink. Fill it up with water, leave the wings a while. Why not try? Maybe not in the bathroom. Better to keep the archangel out of the bathroom, something might happen. In the bathroom, besides defecation, unspeakable things sometimes happen.

The archangel got his sword back, it's sad and small, looks like a dagger. The scales are too big, he can barely lift them, Saint Michael might fall on his face. Pitiful.

You won't get lost.

HOW IT HAPPENED

An ad slid under your door says, PUT UP A HAND-RAIL, THE ELDERLY CAN'T STAY STANDING, then you leave the car parked in front of the school where you decided to take refuge for a month that summer, and when you get out of class, there's an ad for handrails and storm door instal-lation. You deduce what anyone with a shred of critical thought would deduce: they've installed handrails. What you can't figure out is where. But if they did it, they minimized risk. That night you fall asleep a little less sad.

Days before, you spot a car with a skull bumper sticker. Death says hello again, it's all around you, wants to sink its teeth into your jugular. You can't see inside the car, the windows are tinted.

•

María listens and says she agrees, it's terrible everywhere now. Her inscrutable blue eyes observe you. You talk to her about the Masons. She responds:

"Ah, so you think the Masons will be a thing again."

•

When you wake up, the usual happens: You wonder if the thousands of murdered souls are already gone. You've concluded in earnest that these days any strength that's around is fed by the souls of the dead. If you ventured to describe your body's trances, you would say: Invisible powers tear off my clothes, they climb up my back one after the next. I lock the door, but they slip in through cracks, they've resolved to take everything: The furniture is the least of it, they're hungry and go for the fruit, the ham, the yogurt; their bruised mouths gobble it all. Nothing satisfies them, soon they'll eat me alive.

You remember one meal with María, where

you told her: There are actors everywhere. She laughed and said back:

"Poor nobodies, they've got nothing better to do."

Who are they? María is right, they're no one. Bodies manipulated by other bodies manipulated by the most powerful body of all, trying to pass for something else.

You turn your attention to your heart and feel its postwar flesh is frozen.

•

The terror you feel in the face of violence is almost another person, another body beside you, it's your double.

•

The substance is a splint for the emotions. The most critical points, descending triangles, are held in place so the soul line slopes downward as little as possible. A lesser curve. The neurons keeping pace. But all the same, there's a descent; a deepening immersion in the wells: identity is rebellious and will only extend its journey if some substance tries to appease it. It's a ploy.

•

Could it have started thousands of years ago? It'd make no difference if the explanation of events began with bones found at one of the poles. Human bones. A woman who looks at another woman and wants her to disappear, that kind of thing. The skeleton of a prehistoric woman buried deep in the snow.

You think it's important to document events.

Writing as testimony. Although what happens isn't true. Almost nothing can be considered true. Writing isn't true either.

With a disordered imagination, it turns out that retelling the same sequence of events again and again is actually vital. You hope someone understands. From a psychoanalytic perspective, you're probably setting limits, scooping the spilled water into

buckets so there's no ground rot. Avoiding putre-
faction at all costs. Psychoanalysis takes a feeble
view of existence. Words spoken return to your
head like birds you wounded yourself.

You've lost too much already. What follows will
only come by way of the spirit. You want to pray.
You've thought about going to church and even
becoming a nun, pleading for others and yourself.
Begging God. Please, you say, teeth clenched, as if
with one word you could let slip the most shameful
sense of your circumstance: May a higher power be
so benevolent as to save you, because you, so often,
feel you no longer can. A part of the thought splits
off and tumbles into the abyss: Nothing means
anything, we humans are shit animals careening
toward the end. We'll go back to eating each other,
humans devouring humans, until not one bone is
left with a shred of meat.

•

By the time she left the city, she'd lost weight.
Wasn't hungry, was alone in a borrowed

apartment. The storms and plagues had already happened. Millions of floods. Extinct species, dark thoughts.

•

Your friend is worried. Says she heard from informants that a ghost had been living with you. Really, she sounds uneasy: "It's freaky shit," she says. A ghost. If there was a ghost, it must have been because someone was dead but close to you, or close to him, your partner during that year so heavy with meaning it still isn't over. There are times that sink their hooks into our bodies, episodes sucking blood from the backs of our knees, from the crooks of our arms, where the veins show. That's what your friend is talking about. About you, not herself like you'd thought.

•

There was a room in the house full of suitcases left behind by the people who passed through. It was silent. The only recurring murmurs were of the water that ran through the pipes, and in winter, the whistling of hot radiator foil.

A massacre took place there. Something so sinister that it showed up on many people's tongues. What happened? What event, which body, what ghost? Your chest trembles when you consider the possibilities; here comes your imagination, bearing its fangs, it sinks them into your body.

It's a serious matter. Think about it. Repeat: It's a serious matter and must be treated as such. A ghost in a house. A ghost living with a couple that's in love. In bed, the ghost lies between them, it's very slender then, it slips right in, takes the shape of the sleeping bodies, grazes their sleeping contours, kisses their foreheads. When they make love, the ghost stands under the doorframe to watch, levitates, excited, as it registers what's happening.

It's one ghost. Or are there several? The informant has stated that there's just the one. Female or male? Bear in mind that in some cases, the flesh and blood are classified as ghosts. Though it's unlikely they're describing a living person. They're talking about a dead person who inhabited a house where you were lost in love. Perhaps the ghost ate off your plate when you weren't looking, a moment of carelessness, just there, while you refilled the pitcher, it ate off your plate and left its acid saliva on your fork. He didn't notice, certainly, or if he did, he kept quiet about it. Your memory summons three photographs to your eyes, they form a sequence: the couple walking hand in hand on a beach; then the couple running, not letting go, fingers clenched so the hands make a knot; and finally, they leap over the sand to fall further.

·

The day before you left, you took the bus to see the ocean for the last time. You stood before it and it was frenzied, so in tune with your interior.

·

Huge waves surpassed the heads of the onlookers, witnesses to the marine phenomenon. It was bizarre. In front of you was a photographer with his tripod pressed into the sand, agape at the spectacle.

You said goodbye. I'll come back when conditions are better. And that was it.

Now the ghost glides across the floors of another house. Stones, golden horseshoes, animal vertebrae, none of it offers protection to those tenants either. The ghost drinks water from a glass where there's a trace of your red lips.

THE BEAUTY OF LIGHT
IS YOUR FACE

Your stare empties into a white candle on the coffee table. Peace could be distilled to a candle like that. This is where time turned to stone, you think. If peace is a fragment of time in memory, you want to keep it. You see her with scales in her left hand, a sword in her right, that's how it was, her standing just in the center of the room, on the night before her departure. Then you get up and walk to the window, heart beating hard. You're observing the lean of the sink when out of nowhere, her figure appears in the air. Gradually she materializes before you. Her body is translucent. You can see, on the other side of it, the corner of the courtyard, the water heater. She's wearing a red sweater over a dress with small flowers on it. Turns the tap and fills a deep clay dish, then wets the garment stretched over the rippled wash-board, grabs a bar of soap, and works it against the fabric. You look at the ground in hopes of clear-ing your vision; when you look back toward the courtyard, she's still there, now rinsing the gar-ment. In a flash you're outside in the midday sun, she's right there, a meter in front of you. You step closer and reach out to touch her shoulder. Your hand crosses through her body. And then her image vanishes, as abruptly as it appeared.

You go back inside, close the metal door, and look back at the washbasin from the living room, wondering if you just saw her there, standing, or if you only imagined it. There's no way of knowing.

•

After eating the egg with a little salt, pepper, and lime, she throws the shell in the trash. She washes the cup she used as a bowl and puts it on the dry-ing rack. Doesn't realize she left the burner on.

She stops in the kitchen doorway and looks at her hands. At that moment, her thinking has long, twisted roots. Butterfly tongues sprout from her fingers. She no longer recognizes her hands, or rather, the hands she sees had been hers, yet now she extends them and feels a heaviness, perceives them as another woman would, receiver of hands she didn't know. There are no stitches on her wrists. How were these hands affixed to her body? It's a mystery.

Her nose crinkles as if, in the air in the house, she's picked up on something acidic. For a moment, it seems like she stops breathing. The only suitcase she's taking with her is waiting by the door. You never know where a trip will take you.

Actually, the transit started before that, early one morning, when prehistoric figures appeared on one of the walls. Between two bookshelves, above the paint blisters, she saw a perfect imprint of a hand, and an inch or so above, the outline of a buffalo. Or so she thought. She placed her hand on the imprint and confirmed they were the same size. But she had never dipped her hand in any paint and pressed it there. She thought to scratch at the paint blister, never imagining that, at the touch of her fingernails, the wall would begin to exude or emit an amberish liquid, like tree sap. She might've said the wall was crying a thick tear. It wasn't water that had pooled in the pores of the concrete and bricks. It was something else. And curiosity led her to collect that drop of concentrated amber and bring it to her mouth. She wasn't worried about being poisoned—this was her own home, after all—nor did she imagine a special trance induced by the substance. It tasted sweet. She stepped back to look at the drawings again, from a distance. How strange, what are they trying to say, she thought. Shrugged as if to tell herself that, though baffling, the occurrence was harmless. She placed no importance, for example, on the tiny portrayal of a buffalo.

At night, in the deepest abyss of her sleep, something else happened. The nonexistent images show her prone body and a bright nebula that slowly issues forth and settles on top of her, then moves through the bedroom toward the door, crosses the living room, hovering all the time half a meter above the ground, and reaches

the front door. There, it stops, and thanks to
the light from the hallway, the haze shines even
brighter, a mound of glitter hanging in the air.
One window is open. The haze passes through it
and leaves the house.

•

She remains asleep and dreaming, room still
dark, although, to tell the truth, it will brighten
soon, but now the index finger of her right hand
is glowing: the residue of the sap the wall exuded
or emitted, and which she tasted.

Out there, when she finally leaves these lodg-
ings, it's waiting for her . . . What? She isn't sure.
An island, maybe. She starts to breathe again, and
after turning the deadbolt, she opens the door and
leaves, but just before fully crossing the threshold,
her body halfway out, she looks left and right to
make sure no one's walking around the courtyard
just then. Places the suitcase on the eroding stone,
turns the key in the lock three times. Leaves her
house. Doesn't look back. There's nobody in the

courtyard. The neighbors are still sleeping, the week hasn't started yet. Arrives at the final door, unlatches it, then pulls the handle. The uneven doorframe grazes the wall she walks through.

It can't be, it can't be.

How do you walk through a wall?

"Where's your grandmother?" your mother asked. Your grandmother was napping in the guesthouse out back, near the garden. You'd just seen her. Suddenly, she appeared in front of you both.

"Weren't you in the guesthouse?" you asked, a touch of fear in your voice.

"That's right, I was," she said. Then she turned away, a teasing smile on her face.

Your mother, eyes like two flames, confirmed: "It's true, she can walk through walls."

THE ROUNDNESS OF AN EGG

ACT I: OFTEN MENTIONED YONDER
THEY DIVIDED THIS WOMAN IN TWO

You absorb. Feast on other people's words. You swell, bulge, and, in the end, you get sick.

You hang on to each look, each suspicion, the voices of virtually everyone who calls you by your name. You wrap yourself up in them, swallow them, devour them, hungry for death.

It takes nerve.

It takes always vomiting up any excess. A few times you manage to: leaning over the toilet and trying to aim the vomit inside. When you fail, you hurry to clean the floor, leave the place like nothing ever happened. You are vile.

The night your mother was dying, the branches of the Martian tree coalesced on the wall, into sharp profiles. The moon was full.

You were born during your mother's Saturn return. They explained that this was the cause of your nostalgia, your profound existential sadness. The sadness of Saturn.

News of mortal illness is the presage of death itself. From it emerges a new temporal measurement we can call a rite. When the rite begins, death arrives. It's true. The sum of months lived in a journey that doesn't entail feet touching the ground, but suspension. The afflicted party floats. The afflicted party can't understand what's happening, may hallucinate things.

•

The man at the front door of the house where you no longer live is carrying a guidebook under one arm. Has greasy bangs stuck to his forehead. Came for you, but you're gone.

•

You want to die. Is your mother's disease yours too?

She gasps. You're on one side of the bed, one of your siblings is on the other.

You resist believing she's dead. Days go by and you wait for her call.

•

You haven't been in this city long; you don't know it very well. You're in a neighborhood in the north, near where you live. Walking down the street alone with no sense of danger. You stop in front of a theater. Pull open the red velvet curtains just inside the door to discover that it's a bar. There aren't many patrons. You decide to sit down and wait for something to happen. Then a tall older man walks through the door. He heads straight for the bar, like he has a plan. Sits next to you, and seeing him up close, you realize the man is your maternal grandfather.

"I live here," he says.

"In Barcelona? How?"

"I live in La Pedrera."

"Gaudí's Pedrera?

Your grandfather buys you a few whiskeys. After two or three, he starts talking about the last time you were together. He was at a facility learning to walk again. Had been in an accident that left him badly injured. Used a walker, could barely cross the patio there, but now your grandfather is living in La Pedrera, what luck!

Someone told you a relative lived there, you tried to find out who, but it was impossible. When you went, the guard at the entrance said he couldn't give you the names of residents.

You agree to have lunch with your grandfather the next day.

•

That afternoon, you walk the streets of El Born. You lost your keys, they said you could get copies there in minutes. So you go with the spares Adelaida, the doorwoman, lent you. Once you have the new set in hand, you decide to peek through a half-open gate, because when you come across a half-open gate, you can't help but look at the house inside. What's in here? you wonder, sticking your nose in. Then a short man pulls the gate open and says it's a very exclusive bar. You ask him to let you in and he does. The place is unbelievable. There are gorgeous antiques and lamps on exotic-wood tables, magnificent paintings on every wall. You go to the back and spot the owner. His hair is glossy, white, with a perfect part right down the middle, his head opens like a book and he tells you he used to have a restaurant in Vitoria, with everything you see here and more, a restaurant with lions in cages.

You leave because it's late, but you'd have liked to stay and talk, he's become your friend.

•

Back home, someone has watered the plants. Your housemate must have done it, she got off work earlier. You remember your Catalan classes and they seem to have happened more recently than they did. Time has run its course, it's been several months since you took that bus and ran into your grandfather at the bar.

EASTER

They left the house early. Your aunt Clementina had hidden Fairbacks chocolate eggs in the yard. The wrappers shone among shrubbery, in the branches of the trees. The goal was to find as many as possible: more eggs, more chocolate. Tracking down a bunny, especially a solid chocolate bunny, was a triumph.

"She's here, the Easter Bunny is here! Get up!" Clementina cried. At Grandmother's house, the Easter Bunny was female.

"What does she look like?" you and your cousin Cristina asked, worked up, biting your lips. "She's short, a little fat, and she zips around everywhere she goes," Clementina said.

The previous days, they had perforated and drained dozens of eggs to paint the shells. The Easter Bunny hid those, too, but you don't remember if there was something sweet inside them, or if they were empty.

•

Grandmother kept river stones on a porcelain plate, and also a small bird's egg, clean and white. When you shook it beside your ear, you could hear something inside. Was it a treasure? A nestling's body, tiny and withered? One afternoon, you took the egg into the bathroom. Hidden there, you squeezed until the shell broke and found only a delicate skin inside.

There was a mantle over the fireplace, and Grandmother kept the Saint Michael right in the middle. Beside him, a tall picture frame, the faces of her children peering out.

The room where you slept had a low ceiling. You stretched out your hands to touch it. The door to your grandmother's bedroom, wood and green glass, looked to you like the gate of a shrine. It opened to the living room, low and narrow, impossible to close, since there wasn't a door.

On a shelf in her room, your grandmother kept a few remedies: Dr. Bell's skin ointment, an orange glass jar with a heart-shaped lid, possibly from the drugstore. All her creams were moisturizing: Oleoderm, Turtle Cream, and Pond's Crema S for her face.

You would slide under heavy wool blankets to sleep on a firm mattress placed atop a concrete base. There was no need to bring along toys, she would find a way to occupy you and Cristina, or any combination of other cousins.

Next to the fireplace, where your grandmother had placed a smooth, beautiful river rock, lived a statue of an owl. It was an unusual owl, its body long, its face prehistoric and chiseled in gray stone. Sometimes you would take the owl to bed with you, tuck it in, but it barely ever warmed up.

Grandmother would wake up at six in the morning to meditate. Twice she asked you to join her, so you could understand. Simply observe your thoughts, she'd say, and try to think of nothing. Imagine a colorless wall. She sat on cushions upholstered in white rabbit fur. Like thrones.

Would wrap two blankets around her, and give you one, too. Close your eyes, she'd instruct. All the house's mirrors were concealed by gauzy Indian fabrics. Grandmother was terrified of mirrors. That was around the time she gave you the coral-and-turquoise earrings she'd brought from India.

•

Her interest in the Yoga Center started in the sixties. The master, as she called him, was Swami Pranavananda Saraswati. The Swami's fleshy lips were always twisted into a crooked smile. His jet-black eyes sat over heavy dark circles. His skin also glistened, anointed with sweat. At the center, disciples would often present him with floral garlands. The meetings there lasted a very long time.

Are you scared? you would ask your mother during the silences, when you could tell she was deep in thought. She spent many minutes absorbed. What was she thinking of?

The week before she died, your mother wanted to wear the jade ring you gave her. But her fingers were too swollen, it no longer fit.

·

If your soul left your body, it has to come back. Soon, it will.

After you've witnessed the death, you find a moment of contentedness in solitude, in distance from daily spaces. But only a moment, and then there's another, of dread.

It hurts too much. You stop writing.

Tonight, you wait for hail. You go outside to listen to the wind. In a metal chair in the garden, you smoke a cigarette, at the end of it, you feel something small and alive on your arm, turn, and meet the shining eyes of a field mouse who has climbed onto you without warning. You scream. The mouse flees immediately, almost vanishing into thin air. It was quick to arrive, quick to leave. An animal that appears and then disappears, just like language.

•

Talk about the forked language. With other people sometimes something supremely strange happens to you. You notice language forking. Others talk, and in their words, there lurks another meaning, latent. As if they want to say something they won't directly state. What makes this perception peculiar is that often what's not expressed—or not indicated in words—contains a kind of judgement. What does that mean? Or, more precisely, what does it not mean? You wonder.

You dreamed about a heartbeat. Could you be finding one here?

Look how many people have lined up behind you, in search of a little airtime on the phone at the twenty-four-hour store. Airtime. It makes some sense: the words others use on their calls, so we can understand at least something of everyone else.

•

Once, two years ago, a man asked for your email address and wrote to you. Said he was fixing the water leaks at your grandmother's house. His message meant something it didn't articulate but described water leaks in a building and also said he was writing to tell you goodbye. He wrote well, you remember, clipped his sentences, left them unfinished. This is true.

•

If a man asks you to give him money for his daughter with liver disease—on a street you know well, the encounter surprises you—he's asking for spare change so a bomb doesn't drop. If you see two women pushing strollers on the same street, it's sign of a giant mirror that reflects you thousands of times, sends your image off to a satellite, brings it back as something else. The return is unrelenting. It's also likely they're extracting your guts to examine them, they'll always find something useful. People's lives are used in twisted control processes, it's a fact. You hold your hands over the fire, above the terrible flame, and you say: it's a fact.

If you're able to read a message on the horizon, something that includes the words "handrail" and "death," it's a death threat. Later, it could be confirmed in the form of a flyer for aluminum works, which you'll find left on your car's windshield.

Field mice are hiding in other voices.

NO ONE IS NORMAL UP CLOSE

Exercising doesn't mean moving your body to support healthy biological mechanisms. Not anymore. Exercising means not killing and not stealing. And ecology is actually a pestilent, fly-ridden tank, full of personal stories that, made universal, rot at unthinkable speeds.

•

Incessantly watching the corners of his and her lips, to see if there's still a trace of old mother's milk there. Detaching from your own lips to fill them with substances that make them fleshier.

Ask for milk. Call the wet nurses. Hurry.

•

The hand that shakes when it picks up the phone, scratches the tear duct of one cloudy eye, and says: I'm not interested.

•

We'll record all your conversations.
No one is normal up close.

•

We'll buy everything you stand for. Your own life for our own use.
No one believes in anything. Not even their own skin under a sheet mask.

•

The shelves at the supermarket are empty. We want more. For them to give us the full yield of the earth and the factories. For them to grant us universes of cheese, legume superhighways, fill our mouths so we can vomit later at home, at length, kneeling before the toilet.

(It's highly likely that if you read about an accident in a book and then go outside, the accident will come after you. There are too many of us. Let's put meaning out of its misery. We can't speak even in gibberish. There's nothing left.)

Let them take photos of all our body parts, let's trade them and salivate over everyone else's: I want that abdomen; I want his legs, straight and tall; I want her deep, narrow navel.

•

Right. I can't, in fact, share with you what I'm thinking, that's why I'm approximating, in writing, what I want to share with you. I also avoid the word *shadow*. If you put your lover's ear in the mail today, it'd be a metonym. We no longer understand words as we did before. May they be replaced with a piece of the body. Replaced with a jar of mayonnaise.

They'll buy whatever you signify. What your ancestors have signified. Anything can be bought.

If they're in need of content for political or social commentary, they'll swing by your house, set fire to it, then find all sorts of ways to talk about how everything inside burned. They'll have no qualms whatsoever, and their mouths will overflow with fat, juicy words.

If you strike them as merchandisable, they'll go after you. They'll be merciless.

•

Give a piece of furniture your secrets. A pillow won't do, it might come to life and start talking. Your declarations to the pillow could land you somewhere utterly appalling: there, you'll discern the sickly faces of so many citizens. They'll come into the store after you to buy anything, since you're freely traveling the world, and your freedom has to be paid for by someone else so you don't die, or so your time can still be used to carry out a transaction; he must be buying your time, which he has no other way to experience.

If you catch sight of them, they'll say these days they're doing this or that, but really they're pulling strings you don't see in the hustle of everyday life. They're everywhere. They have eyes more fearsome than you can imagine. Their eyes are infernos adorning their faces, transforming them into masks. It isn't them, they're not what they call themselves, they're the eyes of the universe in a state of disaster.

•

You're thinking about the sum of events, a part of them. The words needed to fully name them don't exist. They never will. Talk, say that up until barely a month ago you didn't know the world, nor the people in it. Ask yourself: Where have I been living since I was born?

Say it strikes you as abominable the way the word became flesh. Disclose: Maybe it was the only possible path. The countless recent dead couldn't be part of the past if the word, if each and every word, weren't charged anew with meaning. When a body is destroyed, the word body fractures and dies.

Mention how you interpret the codes. Say:

I saw a man climb a folding ladder on TV, then I read a newspaper headline that said, gas prices climb, so I concluded that gas represented the potential for upward mobility.

To describe how you crossed from one life to another in the present tense, you have to start a chapter.

It's a state of emergency: several men at different moments, carrying a box.

And all around you were actors. People you'd never seen before passing as someone else or as an extension of themselves.

Eyes placed atop identity.

And suddenly, years later, you saw how that tongue wasn't forked like a snake's anymore, now it was different. Each small happening took on a wide-ranging scope of meaning. It was the renaissance. The silent and sinister genesis of a new era.

The first attendees you saw after the Great Door were two young people: a student who made bombs in his spare time and a woman who spoke to you from a new moment in time. The two of them inaugurated the next bit of the path, where you stood in the thick of the rain, clothes soaked, eyes set on a point no longer so distant.

You move your eyes to your hands. Your grandmother would say that the blotches on the back of them were cemetery flowers.

You've achieved an exhaustion of such intensity that you could sleep without stopping for months. And who knows if you'd wake fully rested: the pain and the exhaustion go back several generations.

•

Peace is a short word. One syllable. Is its reality encoded in its brevity? *Combat* is longer.

•

Why, at a given moment, can the word be suspended from a hook? When it happens, the world seems to stand still. The same events take place again and again, ceaselessly, absurdly. A moment when people speak with the same words. Contagion doesn't mean illness, then, but intention.

•

It's eight fourteen PM on a night that refuses to arrive. Summer keeps this day flourishing: cloudy sky, violet light.

Yesterday, late, you found clues that pertained to part of the story you're trying to tell. The plot includes a party in honor of Saint Michael, thrown by the poet Eunice Odio, which may have been attended by a man who, months later, was accused of killing John F. Kennedy: Lee Harvey Oswald. Your grandmother may have been at that party.

Your grandmother was at that party. In fact, it's possible the party wasn't even at Eunice's house.

•

During your research, there came a moment when you set aside the exposé on Eunice Odio's party and looked instead at the Saint Michael you inherited from your mother and your grandmother. You looked at it and wondered if, in fact, that wooden statuette with a tiny sword in its right hand and scales in its left, that archangel your mother had restored because it was missing an arm when it went to her, had powers. If you wished fervently enough, would it come true?

And anyway, what could you ask for?

Don't think about closing your eyes and listening to your grandmother. Then she would decide for you, on something as transcendent as a prayer of petition to an archangel.

•

Secrets. There's a beautiful Eunice Odio poem, "El reflejo," and she dedicates it to your grandmother.

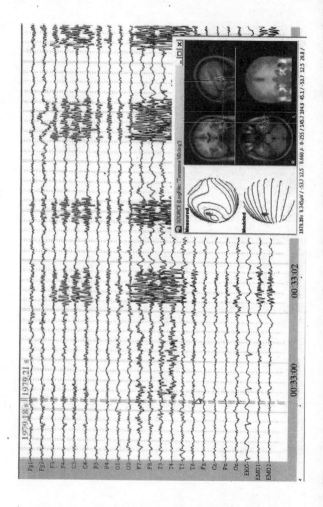

Exhibited persistent hyperarousal in neural circuits controlling passive attention (and anxiety rating), congruence monitoring/encoding, assignment of meaning and valence to stimuli, nociceptive interpretation and response, and ideational integration.

III.

THE WRITER, PURSUED

Once upon a time, a president stole a novel because he considered it dangerous. The author was on the run for years. The president fell in love with the novelist because he was spying on her, and whenever you spy on someone, you're possessed by a deep feeling that resembles, or perhaps is, love. The writer fled from the president. Looked for signals, hidden messages, and found them. Witnessed numerous incidents. For example, in a moment of great distress, terrified and fleeing, she learned that the president was a criminal, one of the worst in history. After that, she heard a woman had died in a distant country and, crazed as she was, thought the death must be linked to her book in some way. No one knows what lines she crosses when she writes.

The writer is hiding out at a friend's house, he's keeping her safe. Because they're following her, but other causes, other reasons, are leading the president, the fearsome criminal, to stalk her, until, one afternoon, she falls to her knees and is stunned to discover a flower emerging from her forehead.

Days pass. The mark of the flower that sprung from her forehead and is now withered is a stigma. She lights candles, prays: "Holy heart of María." Implores her to drive her pursuers away.

The president leaves her alone but sends a lawyer on her domestic flight to tell her she shouldn't give up on publishing her next book. The persecution has been so outrageous that the novel simply must see the light of day.

The president leaves his bedroom and looks for the last time at the photograph of the writer. Her eyes are flames, her hands two fists with special powers; she bears the mark of the flower's emergence on her forehead. The president sticks out his tongue and, with the tip of it, licks the photograph. Then he swallows his saliva, turns and walks to the bathroom, takes a shower.

A day earlier, the president made two phone calls instructing them to destroy all files and recordings pertaining to the writer who was chased across a world without end.

≈

Not one sign remains. You can go out into the street and no one will recognize you. Forgetting is one of power's special abilities.

Calm.

The hours curl up between her legs, a domestic animal.

The stalactites in her brain. The glorious electricity.

·

The woman on the island swallows saliva. It's not so viscous anymore. Hours passed and the word *hunger* remained in her ear, but she'll be satisfied by big mouthfuls of bread and cheese.

Conjuring, she is conjuring, lifting her nose and her chin:

"We still don't call ourselves anything. Our existence has the tongue of a violet serpent.

•

There's a conflagration here.

The dream of our pyromania starts with one of us bringing documents to the fireplace in her house or the sink in her kitchen and burning them up. The burn takes place in secret, like all the most precious things in life. The secret is, flames consume documents, words, and syntax, so sentences veer toward eternity, smolder into ash. Your mother lost an earring or two in the pool. You remember your siblings dove in, they searched all along the bottom so the jewelry would turn up. It did turn up, eventually.

One afternoon, she took you to the pool and said that it was time you learned to swim. Took off your floaties and made you get in. You had sunk to the bottom within seconds and from there you looked up, a silhouette, deformed and blurry; you waited, crouching, and she watched you from above. You did nothing, you were scared. She waited a bit longer. When she saw you had resolved to stay there until she pulled you out, she jumped in and extracted you by the arm. "I was drowning!" you cried after taking a breath. "I can't do it, Mom," you added, lips purple from the cold.

HER BRAIN SCAN

She was lying down. The doctor had left her alone in a half-lit room. If there were a mirror, she'd have seen her own image: a hat with wires coming out of it on her head. Brown tape on the strange wig, electrosensitive; the tape around her waist. The doctor injected gel into one or several orifices in the hat, she felt its viscosity, cold on her scalp. He asked her to lean back and listen to the sounds released by a sweaty machine near the bed. The tones were like a message in morse code. She thought she could decipher it. The machine said: Hey, look up, get out of here, save yourself.

The machine carried on, sometimes releasing shrill cries, other times, moans. She was supposed to distinguish between the two and keep count as well as she could. It's like they're testing my memory, she thought, depleted.

Walls painted white. The door to the hallway:
a possible escape route. Tear off the hat and go, let
the doctor come looking.

"Miss, come back, what are you doing?"

Her back hurts. The flat bed is uncomfortable.
The doctor returns and tells her that now, she'll
see a light over her head. Her eyes have been
closed for half an hour. The light begins to blink,
it's sharp-edged and intense, a knife slicing her
eyeballs into minuscule pieces. In her brain there
are small pulses the wires transmit to the machine
that's breathing beside her. She knows it's reg-
istering every wave emitted by her gray matter
which, though defeated, is rebellious nonetheless.
Her brain says: I won't be broken.

When the light goes out, in the silence barely
touched by the faint buzz of wires, the doctor comes back again. As he closes the door, she
notices he's obsessed with her, nervous, surprised. He asks her to keep her eyes shut. She
does. Why did I come here? she wonders, angry,
uncertain. Who am I? The machine records her
questions in the form of electric pulses, carries

them to the computer the doctor next door is using. That's when it happens. She barely slept the night before, wanting to come to the brain scan in a fragile state of consciousness, and that abruptly prompts her to fall asleep.

•

At that moment she splits in two and leaves her house for the island.

•

She doesn't know how much time passes. The wires tremble on her head, overlong earthworms, ruthless earthworms taking notes on fluctuations in her sleep. The doctor comes in, puts his right hand on her left shoulder, and says: We're all done.

The gray machine, bundle of steel and circuits, lets out a long exhalation.

She gets up slowly, a fragile jellyfish. A larger wire falls along her spine. It's noon on a summer day. The sun has warmed every inch of the office. The doctor slides his fingers between the hat and her forehead, and in a single, precise, studied movement, he strips her of the plastic snakes, at which point they go lifeless. She looks at the flat bed, the hat is there now, and she thinks it resembles a sea creature; the doctor unfastens the tape around her waist.

You can go now, he says. She struggles out of the room. Then the nurse who greeted her at the beginning points to the exit. She pays a good amount of money for the scan, for the snakes. She looks at the clock, the hands show it's twelve thirty. Time to go out into the street. Once she's in the elevator, she realizes one of the serpents is nesting between her breasts. She wants to take it home, put it in a fish tank with stones and little plants, domesticate it.

•

You bring your hands to your eyes, try to see: you think about the inside of your brain. The world is in there. In miniature, artificial lighting and all. The key is in that world, just look at the walls: look at the messages written there, they describe whatever matters most in this moment. Search, scratch the paint, find the symbols and pronounce them, say: Here I read: My time of lamentations has ended, and then, at the bottom, a signature in round strokes. Time has run out, then, on the tiny wall of lamentations. Lift the paint a little so you can get through, leave evidence that you got through on that wall worn by time, sun, and rain.

The universe is expanding. Night will lower its black blanket over a world peopled with ruins and disasters. Between the stones that make the walls, you'll find other letters from your own name, spoken backwards in a strange tongue. Conjure. Lift your nose and chin, conjure: may time exude fruit juice, may you swallow a spoonful of sugar, may you pull the red dress from the closet. Existence has the tongue of a violet serpent, scales that shine in the sun and glow fluorescent in the dark. Sometimes existence looks like a toy from a terrible store.

How do you write the satisfaction of being alive and safe?

You moan, exhale smoke through your nose and your mouth. There's a blaze here. The colors of the blaze don't include orange. May someone attend to the blaze, bear witness to the body that lies in the flames.

•

Your brain scans evaluate the attentional system, affective problems, impulses, persecutory delusions, and the perception of realities others can't conceive of.

EPILEPSY

A woman was flying over our heads. She was in lotus position but she came and went with the crown of her head grazing the ceiling; you think she's around forty, she has short hair, emerald-green pants.

"Will we be able to fly one day, Mom?"

She said yes immediately. Didn't think for even one second. She said: Our minds are very powerful, and with them, we can attain anything.

•

Your mother spent many long hours lying face down in the sun. Napping, maybe. When you got out of the pool, you'd sit on the towel with blue-and-white hexagons, and there, you'd drink the most coveted beverage in the house: Coca-Cola.

At that time, the thing to do was drink it with a squeeze of lime and salt. The saltshaker was on top of the towel, you picked it up over and over, watching the Coca-Cola fizz and taking the perfect swig.

When it's your time for infirmity, your old age, then your death, you'll ask for a nice cold Coke so you can sip on it through a magnificent straw, you'll say: I've always loved Coca-Cola.

In Canaima, Venezuela, the river is the color of Coca-Cola.

•

Your grandmother was set on swimming in the waters of the Orinoco Delta. She wouldn't take no for an answer. "We're already here, I have to get in," she said over and over. There were piranhas, but she wasn't worried anything would happen. She went out onto the riverbank and, shrieking with laughter and joy, invited you all to do the same. There, Cristina (your cousin), the other Cristina (your aunt), your grandmother, and you were baptized right in the Orinoco. That was after a terrifying journey in a piragua. María de la Asunción, your other aunt, the two Cristinas, your cousin Eva, and you had gone out for a ride in the long, slender boat. The water was only an inch from the top. Up front was a Warao man who rowed with ease on the wide, calm river. Suddenly your grandmother stood up and started to dance, she gleefully shook her hips. The boat moved with her, you all did. Olga was resolved to fall in, and to take the rest of you, too.

"No, Grandma!" shouted your cousin Cristina.

"Don't!" was your contribution.

But Olga kept dancing, dying of laughter. Your aunts didn't know if they should shout at her or keep quiet, so they said things like "But . . . Olguita, come on!" gentle, a little afraid. The man was laughing too. Seeing that she had caused real hysteria, she went back to her place and sat down, but first, she told you all that you were the silliest, most boring women she'd met in all her days.

•

Your mother had stopped at the front door. The neighbor came and opened it. You aren't sure why your mother went to that house, but it must have been to have a conversation. While they talked, you entertained yourself by hopping up the stairs to the door. And then you fell. Your mother said: That's what you get for jumping.

Your mother died eight months ago. Those last days, her eyes were bigger. Against the thinness of her face, they jutted outward: two enormous lamps. They seemed to radiate fear; they held her rage at too early a death.

The doctor's face, to the naked eye, told stories like yours. You talked for two hours. It's likely that the substance was causing excessive happiness, but the conversation—in the midst of pain—was happy. You left with your arms stretched out toward the sky. Walked through the hospital halls like that, with the expression of someone surrendering herself to higher powers. You took communion. Fingers extended, gaze forward, strangely proud. Legs bending at the knee to take triumphant steps. The people around you—patients and relatives, doctors—turned to look, waiting for you to explain why you were holding your arms like that. What's she doing? they wondered. Out on the street, you kept your arms up, offered them to the fresh air. I've been given a gift and I'm grateful, you murmured, laughing as you had in your complicity with the doctor. What happened while you spoke is so sacred you won't describe it. A precious space in time where you can see the lines on your hands as grooves in the earth where green moss springs up. Regeneration.

Certain transformations of the soul take place imperceptibly. Voice gets louder, legs get stronger, heart pumps more blood. On the other side, beyond the one hundred and seventy-nine borders you've crossed in your thoughts, you recover your body, then your soul: it returns through your mouth, warms your trachea, hits your stomach where it makes air sounds before it descends to your womb to gestate a tingling reconception. You hadn't believed you would ever breathe with an unsevered soul again.

The memories scatter. The image is: a drop of oil that falls into water. You can't gather up what happened inside of you, impulses and anguish so primitive they resist language, twist, flee. They become unpoppable bubbles, as if reenforced with steel.

But it isn't late or early, the present is forcefully living. The present breathes over your mouth, leaves behind a mist fragrant with flowers.

•

At your mother's wake there were flowers. Roses, mostly. Arrangements sent by friends of the family. Now when you think of her in the coffin, it feels like a scene from a movie you saw. Pure illusion. You don't know if you actually experienced that night, or the months preceding her death. When the person "on her death bed" is someone you love, the phrase bleeds and suddenly warns of your own demise: when the person is someone you love, you're on the next bunk over.

You keep thinking about things she lived through that you didn't, when she was sick and in the hours before she died. Because you had wanted to share those last months with her in every way, but you couldn't, that was impossible. Fragility is also a manifestation of ego.

Doesn't writing about her death, about her

condition, make you a vulgar person? Say you're alive, does that give you some privilege over the dead?

·

A few days ago, while you were talking with Fabiola, you wore a necklace you had inherited from your mother. You told her about it, knowing this friend always sees deeper. You kept talking and then, in a flash, it broke and the amethysts scattered.

It's Tuesday. Summer is a bit late this year. You're wearing a tank top. Since yesterday you've been nervous: in a few days you'll get the results of the brain scan.

·

You've read the results. You're not normal.

You go along blindly, describing what you feel, what you see. In your situation it's impossible to know if what you're writing is for better or for worse. Then you wait, watch the ripples on the surface of the water, sleep away a life, anesthetize a thought, give in without even realizing it.

Here several men in bowler hats are carrying a box.

That happened because you looked somewhere else.

The word suspended from a hook.

THE HEN WITH A SCAR
ON ITS HEAD

THE WORLD'S ANIMALS WERE A robotic creation. One was a dog so small people found her disgusting; her eyes sought you out from the foot of your bed on the night of the wedding. You drove her from your room as if she were the devil's personal envoy. Had heard her howling a few hours earlier, whining, too, like she knew what you were thinking. It was only the two of you in the house, since the party was being held somewhere nearby. The guests were already squealing.

The next morning you saw a sinister hen, its face crossed with a fleshy scar: you thought the factory must have branded it. The older dogs weren't real, their snouts were tin cans covered in fur, adrip with glycerin drool. On the horizon, volcanoes rose in skeins of clouds; not a single summit could be seen.

It was two on the dot when the man in the overcoat approached you. Soon after, the two of you went up the mountain, it looked like the sun was about to rise even though it was fully afternoon. You came back alone, your stomach a fistful of acids. You walked upon the too-fine powder of the path, you skirted the monastery, and the powder looked like cocaine covering half your legs. The skies boomed, warning of water, and you thought again that a great eye was looking down on you: miniscule, crossing the forest, crying electric shame.

•

You forgave your grandmother when you remembered how happy you felt on those early mornings, leaving the house, cold biting your cheeks, to see if the hen had laid eggs.

HER CLEANSING

IN A ROOM WITH A man who's holding her head as he prays to God, to the gods, to all gods, implores them to purge "this child, the body of this child" of her jealousies. Around them walks a young boy who will later smile at her in the drugstore, when she goes to buy potato chips. The boy circles them, shaking a cowbell, or something similar to a cowbell. Across from her is an altar crowded with saints. A stone on the ground stained slightly red. The man waves a bundle of dried herb-of-grace over her body, pauses at her spine and at her calves. She wants them to go. And squeezes her eyes shut so as not to see what's there, standing in front of the altar. She would have preferred not to hear the man, either—his voice was too unpleasant.

Afterward, he throws alcohol on the ground

and lights it on fire, then uses a rag to smother the flames.

He takes an egg and rolls it over her back, her waist, her knees, then gives it to her, takes her hands that are holding the egg, and guides them to her chest. A moment later, he asks her to give back the egg so he can crack it on the lip of a glass and empty it into water. The truth appears in the grayish albumin.

•

How does a person catch the devil's eye?

•

The man, who has buttoned his lab coat up to the hollow between his collar bones, tells her she needs three more sessions.

His assistant is no longer there. Before leaving, he grinned at her with his baby teeth.

THE WOMAN WHO LEFT FOR THE ISLAND WAS YOU

THE PREVIOUS AFTERNOON, STANDING OUT in the courtyard, in front of the washbasin, you felt her presence again. Turned to look for her: she would often wander the house and only show herself after sunset—her contour was bluish, it sometimes had the consistency of moss occupying the air—and you would discover that a fine powder, also blue, had settled on the furniture and carpet.

That afternoon she did something different, because you felt a slight pain in your shoulder, as if you'd been pricked with a needle. Then you saw the thinnest ring of light sprout from your shoulder and move toward the living room door. It was probably an extension.

Even at the port, you felt a stinging in that

same shoulder. Maybe she had managed to cross through your body for the first time.

Another unusual aspect of her last appearance that afternoon: you could see, in the glass of the window that opened to the courtyard, the reflection of her head, scalp glistening under the living-room lamp. Her lack of hair is mimicry too, you thought. What she wants now, because she thought of it and can, is to look like someone with cancer.

•

How will you die on the island, exactly? You could feasibly list possibilities, one of them common: your breathing will shut down and your heartbeat will slow until you draw your final breath and your face contorts in a terrible grimace, like you've just swallowed a brew so bitter that it strikes you down. It must be your stomach acid, plus the pills.

•

Three or four days before your mom died, you said: If you want to scream, scream. She was sitting on the edge of the bed, palms of her hands on the mattress. Looking at the ground. Not crying. She was too weak to cry. How, then, would she have screamed?

Outside the wind is blowing so hard you might see your cabin torn from the ground and into a twister.

•

Free souls try to exert control so as not to die of fright.

The following statements are true:

a. Your grandmother didn't walk through the wall of your house.

b. El Camarón (your grandmother's yoga instructor, the Swami) was a con man dressed in orange.

c. The most fearsome events happen quietly.

d. The electrical pulses in your brain's nucleus are normal.

e. The woman did, in fact, die on the island. And before she arrived, she noticed, amid a perfectly natural panic attack, a rocky islet shaped like an iguana.

f. The blue powder she left on your furniture was true.

g. No one witnessed you tasting the liquid that oozed from the wall of your house, where you found the outline of a small buffalo and the handprint.

h. The man taking cardboard boxes up to the roof saw her leave.

i. The blimp she saw in the air, on which she read COCA-COLA, really existed.

j. If money is exchanged, people die.

k. You have your grandmother's Saint Michael. Others who revered him included Eunice Odio, Amparo Dávila, and Elena Garro.

l. You found out about their friendship after your grandmother was dead.

m. If a man with thin, greasy bangs shows up at your house with a guidebook under one arm, don't open the door.

n. Life is everlasting, it has no death.

o. There once was a tree, and it was real.

p. They left you a ring with an emerald and two diamonds. It must be your only inheritance. And you said: It's not really me.

q. They say your grandmother had lots of jewelry and your mother and siblings pawned it and lived for years off the money they made.

r. There are writings that make you a better person and there are other writings.

s. The mouse that climbed up your arm that time was a reincarnated relative.

t. There's no reason this list has to include every letter of the alphabet.

Right now, the woman on the island is thirsty, she has never needed water more intensely, but she can't drink it: she has none, and what's more, she has resolved to extinguish her days there. On the horizon, she sees a burst of seawater expelled by a gray whale. She has on blue underwear and no shirt. A few hours ago she ingested the pills and already they burn her insides: a bitter taste climbs her esophagus to her tongue; the middle of her forehead stings as if subcutaneous pins were spreading, little by little, from there to her nose and cheeks. Her eyes burn from the sun and the sweat. In the trances, her vision distorts, and she thinks she can see the trajectory of the light.

She has been sitting on the shore. Now, she allows for her body's first abdication: lies down, arms over her head, and crowns herself with her interlaced fingers. Maybe because of that movement, she becomes aware of a stabbing in her bladder and she yields: she urinates on the sand, for the first time since she got to the island six hours ago. The last liquids she consumed were a coffee and an orange juice at her breakfast by the port.

Now she looks toward the sky. No clouds fill the space where she's looking, since they're gathered on the horizon, right at the edge of the sea. She keeps her arms above her head, and abruptly, it begins: Her feet fall open, the left one starts moving. It first seems triggered by a nerve impulse, then it is thrown into spasms. The woman doesn't unclasp her fingers. Something takes hold. She's losing herself, leaving; death speeds up as she savors an unspeakable bitterness, she presses her tongue to her palate and breathes out hard through her nose, as if clearing thick black smoke from her nostrils, but the air in that moment is shining. A witness would have seen filaments of light sprouting from her chest, ascending, and would also have seen her speaking a word, her last. Her eyelids fall shut and it looks like they've always been there, eyes closed like mouths that don't open, lids stitched shut with fishing line.

She feels a cracking in her abdomen, something bursts, she writhes a little, but her hands remain on her crown. Then she experiences an interior tearing, perceives, with absolute clarity, her enervated organs, which jettison liquids and fats.

It's her. This is her.

An almost black liquid reaches her mouth. Here, approaching the hereafter, her mouth reflects her body's will and makes a slug of the liquid, her shriveled tongue fumbles then allows it to dribble slowly from the edge of her right lower lip: it's as if her mouth is crying.

With minimal movement, her hands uncross, free from their former diligence. Her closed eyes roll back as far as possible. Ligaments tear. Her dislocated eyeballs are free in their sockets.

Convinced of the presence of witnesses, she opens her blackened lips and inhales. The gesture is shared between her last mouthful of air and first instant of death. She exhales through her nose, extinction begins.

END OF THE WORLD

She died after an illness reduced her body mass to seventy-seven pounds.

She couldn't breathe. Her lungs were fibrous, her heart weak. She reached old age.

She split without realizing. Ended her days on an island.

But you, your heart will grow until it springs from your mouth. That's your calling and your yearning, and it will become your reality.

·

The jacaranda's thousand lilac eyes looked on as your mother died.

October 4, 2014. You're about to fall asleep, and your mother appears in your eyes, and then in the world, in reality. She speaks and gestures, lives. She goes with you. What is she saying? You don't know, but she's moving her hands in the usual way. Her body occupies space.

Now let those fears pass, remain at a distance. Don't let them find another body here.

Say: You went too soon, Mom, or I got here late.

•

Before she ingested the pills, the woman on the island walked along the shore. The gulfweed described the edge of the beach and stretched meters into the water, like orange foam. She sank her feet into the algae. Stopped when she saw a red plastic bottle caught in its soft branches. Not far from there, on the walls of the continent's pre-Hispanic ruins, tiny living shells clung to stone and others were buried in sand.

They had told her that a few kilometers out, surrounded by sea, was an island of plastic: an accumulation of garbage. It's a grotesque island of colors. If she were to swim among the containers, the shards of plexiglass, she could convey the way they've transformed. Their sheen—their most attractive feature—must be lost, as with the bottle she found; the salt and the drag of the sea would have turned the debris opaque.

·

From the window in the study, you see the tree, its metallic leaves. At its foot, a star-shaped shadow on the ground. It is neither too early, nor too late. This world has reached its conclusion.

Silence. She's here, behind a closed door framed by interior light.

Signal Amplitude

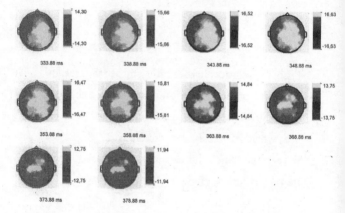

Areas of hyperexcitability during non-paroxysmal periods (LORETA) at anterior dorsal angle, bilateral septum and gyrus rectus, upper-left rostral frontal region, and right amygdala.

AUTHOR'S NOTE

The images appearing in this book are from the Electroencephalogram Spectral Analysis and Event-Related Potentials I had done in May 2014. The accompanying text is taken from the findings and medical interpretations of this analysis.

I'm grateful to Blanca Gaxiola, psychiatrist, and Montserrat Gerez, neuropsychiatrist, for helping me understand my brain's excessive electrical discharges. And to Guy Pierre Tur for helping me balance the sun.

Daniela Tarazona (Mexico City, 1975) is the author of *El animal sobre la piedra* (Mexico, Almadía, 2008, and Argentina, Entropía, 2011), forthcoming in English as *The Animal on the Rock* from Deep Vellum. In 2012, she published her second novel, *El beso de la liebre* (Alfaguara), which was shortlisted for the Las Américas Prize in 2013. In 2020, the book *Clarice Lispector: La mirada en el jardín* (Lumen) was published, co-written by Tarazona and Nuria Mel. Her work has been translated into English and French. She has been a fellow of Mexico's Young Artists program and is currently a member of the FONCA fund's National Network of Artists. In 2011, she was recognized as one of twenty-five Latin American literary secrets by the Guadalajara International Book Fair. In 2022, she received the prestigious Sor Juana Inés de la Cruz Prize for *Divided Island*.

Lizzie Davis is a translator, writer, and former senior editor at Coffee House Press. Her recent translations include Juan Cárdenas's *Ornamental* (a finalist for the 2021 PEN Translation Prize) and *The Devil of the Provinces*; Elena Medel's *The Wonders*, cotranslated with Thomas Bunstead; and work by Valeria Luiselli, Pilar Fraile Amador, and Daniela Tarazona.

Kevin Gerry Dunn is a ghostwriter and Spanish/English translator whose book-length projects include *Easy Reading* by Cristina Morales (for which he received an English PEN Award and a PEN/Heim Grant) and work by Paul B. Preciado, María Bastarós, Elaine Vilar Madruga, Ousman Umar, Daniela Tarazona, Javier Castillo, Paco Cerdà, and Cristian Perfumo.